GUTTERSNIPE

Jane Cutler
Pictures by Emily Arnold McCully

Farrar Straus Giroux
New York

For my cousin, Janet Fried —J.C.

Text copyright © 2009 by Jane Cutler
Pictures copyright © 2009 by Emily Arnold McCully
All rights reserved
Distributed in Canada by Douglas & McIntyre Ltd.
Color separations by Chroma Graphics PTE Ltd.
Printed and bound in the United States of America by Phoenix Color Corporation
Designed by Jonathan Bartlett
First edition, 2009
10 9 8 7 6 5 4 3 2 1

www.fsgkidsbooks.com

Library of Congress Cataloging-in-Publication Data
Cutler, Jane.
    Guttersnipe / Jane Cutler ; pictures by Emily Arnold McCully.— 1st ed.
        p. cm.
    Summary: In Canada early in the twentieth century, Ben, the youngest in a family of Jewish immigrants struggling to make ends meet, decides to help out but when a hat maker gives him a chance, disaster strikes and Ben nearly loses hope.
    ISBN-13: 978-0-374-32813-9
    ISBN-10: 0-374-32813-7
    [1. Hope—Fiction. 2. Responsibility—Fiction. 3. Poverty—Fiction. 4. Immigrants—Fiction.
5. Jews—Canada—Fiction. 6. Canada—History—1867–1914—Fiction.] I. McCully, Emily Arnold, ill.
II. Title.

PZ7.C985 Gut 2009
[E]—dc22

2007034417

AUTHOR'S NOTE

A long time ago, before World War I, my father lived in a city in Canada that had large, beautiful parks, with greenswards and gardens and stately trees. At the entrances to the parks were signs that said "No Jews or Dogs Allowed."

My father didn't know about the signs. He never went to the parks. He lived with other Jewish immigrants in the poorest parts of that city, where people had to work day and night for next to nothing, and many felt a little lost and longed for relatives and friends, cities and towns they had left behind, far across the ocean.

But my father was a child of the New World and longed only for what was ahead. In his heart of hearts, he believed he was meant to have a different—and a better—life. He was determined not to live in poverty forever. And he was full of hope.

As it turned out, my father had the good life he dreamed of. But he did once tell me about a day when he came very close to losing heart and losing hope. And that's the day that inspired this story.

After Ben's papa died, there was never enough money. Mama could not find a way to make ends meet. So Anna, Ben's older sister, who was a milliner's apprentice, got a second job selling tickets at a movie theater. And Max, Ben's older brother, quit school to work full-time. Mama worked as many extra hours at the clothing factory as the boss would allow. And when two greenhorn cousins arrived from the old country, smelling oniony and lost, Mama agreed to let them sleep on cots in the kitchen and use the stove and pay her whatever they could.

Still, there was never a penny left over.

Ben decided he had to get a job, too.

Ben's friend Avram told him that Mr. Green, the hatmaker, was looking
for a boy to work after school.

He ran all the way to Green's.

"You're little," said Mr. Green. "How old are you?"

"Twelve," Ben lied.

"You're skinny."

"I'm strong," Ben argued.

"I don't know."

"Let me try," Ben insisted.

"Wait here," the man finally said.

Then he went and got an old bike that had a woven basket attached to its handlebars. Inside the basket Ben saw stacks of silk circles, hundreds of circles, in many different colors.

"These are hat linings," said Mr. Green. "You sew them inside the tops of men's hats and caps."

On one finger, he held up a gold-colored circle for Ben to see.

Even in that dim and dust-filled office, the silk circle magically caught whatever light there was. Ben stared at it.

"I need a boy to take hat linings to my factory on the other side of Hill Street," Mr. Green said. "That's the job. Five cents for every trip."

Ben was still staring at the shining circle.

Mr. Green put it back into the basket. "Five cents," he repeated. "If you want to give it a try, you can take a load right now and then come back." He balanced the hat linings in the basket, pushed the bike out onto the sidewalk, and watched as Ben mounted it and wobbled away.

Once Ben got used to the bike, he sailed along. Riding with the breeze at his back made him feel strong and free. He thought about the gold circle, shining like a promise. Then he grinned and jiggled the handlebars to make the basket shake. A basket full of promises! he thought.

To get to Hill Street, Ben had to pass the bowling alley where his brother Max and Max's pal Rudy worked. The back door was open and he stopped to listen to the heavy balls rolling down the wooden lanes, hitting the pins and knocking them over. He could see Max working like crazy, setting up the fallen pins and then scrambling out of the way as the ball came toward them.

"Not everybody can be a pinboy," Max had bragged after his first day of work. "You've got to be fast. You've got to be tough. You've got to have your wits about you. A guy could get hurt back there."

Max was quick. He had his wits about him. And he was tough. But Ben remembered how tears had filled his brother's eyes when Mama told him he was going to have to quit school and go to work full-time.

Ben pushed on.

The movie theater was only a block out of Ben's way. He decided to stop by so he could see his sister, even though he knew she couldn't talk to him while she was working. Sitting in the ticket-seller's window, Rose didn't look anything like the dreamy sister Ben was used to. She had her hair piled up on top of her head and she was wearing lipstick and something on her cheeks that made them red, too. She was wearing Mama's glass earrings.

Rose looked like a bright bird in a cage. She sat very straight, waiting to sell tickets. Ben watched for a few minutes. Then he rode on.

The clothing factory where Ben's mother worked was only a few more blocks out of his way. Ben decided to ride by there, too. Mr. Green would not expect him to finish more than one trip on his first day. And he'd make up for it. He really would. He'd work hard every day from now on.

When Ben got to the factory, he could hear the hum of the sewing machines and the thump of the pressing machines and, through a partly open window, he could see his mother. She sat at her sewing machine alongside her friends. Her foot pumped the treadle as her hands skillfully guided cloth under the needle. The women were paid according to how many pieces they could finish, so they worked as fast as they could. And as they bent over their work, they sang.

The sound of his mother and her friends singing together in Yiddish made
Ben feel peaceful and happy. He stayed and listened for as long as he dared.
Finally, he turned the bike toward Hill Street.

So how does a boy get up such a big hill on a bike? Here's how: He waits for a streetcar to come and begin toiling up the long stretch. He checks to be sure the conductor is busy. Then he grabs on to one of the shiny poles at the back, bends over so he's hard to see, and keeps his fingers crossed. Up Hill Street goes the streetcar, and up Hill Street goes the boy. Ben had seen other boys do it, and he was sure he could do it, too. "Easy," he told himself.

Ben hitched a ride on the first trolley that came along. Leaning low, with one hand on the handlebars to steady the basket and the other firmly grasping the brass pole, he sailed along up to the top of the hill. Then he got ready to let go. Not an instant too soon or too late, or the turning trolley would slam him down onto the pavement.

Ben heard the warning screech and felt the streetcar jerk into its turn.
He waited for just the right moment.
He let go.
A split second late.

Down went the bike. The basket tore away from the handlebars, and before
Ben really understood what had happened to him, he saw hat linings spilling
out and spinning across the road. They looked funny! Like hundreds of
children dressed in bright colors, hurrying away. Ben laughed out loud.

Then the angry conductor roared, "Guttersnipe!"

And the instant Ben heard the ugly word, he felt a stabbing pain in his shoulder and understood that nothing was funny and that he was hurt.

Ben lay helpless. He watched the wind swirl hundreds of hat linings around with the rest of the trash in the trash-filled street, driving them into alleys and doorways, gutters and sewers.

What had he done? Mr. Green would be furious. Mama would be so upset. He had wanted to help, but he had only made things worse. Nobody would ever trust him again.

He did not even try to get up.

But then, to Ben's surprise, another wind came rushing up the hill. It swept underneath some linings lying on the ground nearby and blew them into the air right over his head. Magically, there they hung until they got his attention. And then, with the brilliant blue of the sky behind them and the sunlight streaming through, they spun, they whirled, they floated and dipped—red, green, blue, white, black, and golden circles of the finest silk, light as feathers, bright as hope, shining like promises. Hat linings danced above Ben's head.

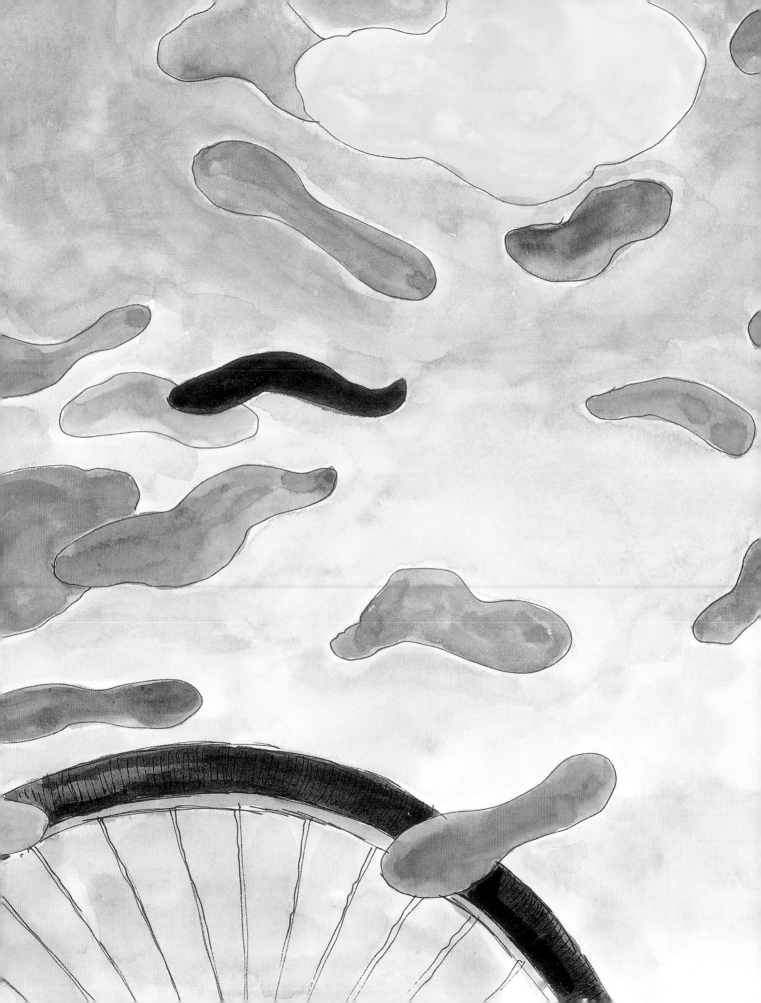

Suddenly, Ben felt that he, too, was rising up into the air, spinning slowly, then faster and faster, rising high—higher—until he was in the midst of the dancers, lofted up by the friendly second wind.

The hat linings surrounded him, tumbling and twirling joyously. Ben was dazzled by the light and the colors and the movement. He could not remember a single sad thing. And in the midst of the dance, this understanding came to him: His body would heal. There would be other bicycles, other jobs, and other chances. He was only a boy, just starting out, and he had many things left to learn and to experience.

This was not the end. This was only the beginning.